Karen Lister.
"Jan 79"

OWL·AT·NIGHT

by Ann Whitford Paul · pictures by Catherine Stock

Macdonald

A MACDONALD BOOK
Published by arrangement with the Putnam Publishing Group, Inc.

Text Copyright © 1985 by Ann Whitford Paul
Illustrations Copyright © 1985 by Catherine Stock

First published in Great Britain in 1987
by Macdonald & Co (Publishers) Ltd
London & Sydney
A BPCC plc company

Printed and bound in Singapore

Macdonald & Co (Publishers) Ltd
Greater London House
Hampstead Road
London NW1 7QX

British Library Cataloguing in Publication Data

Paul, Ann Whitford
    Owl at night.—(Picture book fiction)
    I. Title II. Stock, Catherine III. Series
    813′.54[J]   PZ7

    ISBN 0-356-13512-8
    ISBN 0-356-13513-6 Pbk

For Ron and Sue, thank you A W P

For Niki and Jude C S

The sun, a large orange, is sliced in half and finally disappears. The sky fades to a soft grey and the leaves, once green in the sunlight, darken.
It is dusk, that brief time between day and night.

The owl sleeps peacefully on the branch of a giant oak tree.
Around him everyone is eating dinner.
The rabbit munches on a leaf of lettuce in the garden.
The mother robin divides a fat pink worm among
her babies.

The door of the big house opens so the old dog can
hurry to his bowl.
Inside a girl passes the jug of milk to her brother.

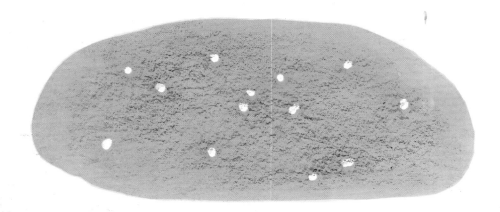

The last patch of grey is gone.
Now the sky and leaves are both so black it is hard to see
where the tree ends and the sky begins. The stars flicker
and the moon seems to hang by an invisible thread.
It is night.
The owl shivers in the chilly air and begins to wake up.
He opens one big round eye and then the other.

The rabbit finishes eating and cleans his paws and face.
The mother robin flutters around the nest,
making her babies cosy and comfortable.
The old dog saunters across the lawn to his kennel.

Inside the house, the children change into
their pyjamas. It is late and they are tired.
The owl spreads his wings and looks around.
'Who-oo Who-oo Who-oo,' he hoots.

The rabbit hops quickly into his hole.
The mother robin stares at the owl as if to say, 'Shh!'
The old dog whines softly.
The children peer out of their window for the owl.
But soon their mother comes. She tucks them in bed and
turns out the light.

Now it is dark. And except for the swish of the oak leaves
swaying in the cool breeze, the night is still.
The rabbit curls up in his snug hole.
The mother robin spreads her wings around her brood.
The old dog turns round and round to
find a spot to lie down.
Inside the house, the boy snuggles his teddy bear.
His sister cuddles up to her doll.

It is time to sleep. But the owl is wide awake.
He hunches his back and twists to fluff and clean
his feathers. Then he watches for other night creatures
beginning to stir.
Suddenly the owl turns his head. A mouse is scurrying
across the grass. The owl swoops down and
glides towards supper. He catches the mouse and
returns to the oak tree.
After eating, the owl explores his world.
He slides between the branches of the mother robin's tree.
He skims over the rabbit's hole.

He flies past the children's window and lands on
the roof of the old dog's kennel.
The owl stares up at the moon and the stars.
Then he breathes deeply and flaps his wings.
He soars through the black sky back to his perch.
'Who-oo Who-oo Who-oo,' he hoots through the night.

The sky lightens and the moon and stars disappear.
It is dawn, that brief time between night and day.

The owl turns his head from side to side as
the world around him wakes up.
The rabbit hops back to the garden.
The baby robins peep for their mother to
bring them another worm.
The old dog yawns and slowly stretches.
Inside the house, the children kick the covers off
their beds.

The sun peeks over the horizon and paints the sky blue.
At last, it is morning.
The owl tightens his grip on the branch and
sways peacefully.
The rabbit nibbles a carrot.
The baby robins chirp eagerly for their mother's return.
The old dog scratches at the door of the big house.
Inside, the girl kneels to tie her brother's shoelace.

The sun floats higher and higher.
Its rays dance through the cotton wool clouds,
and the oak leaves glisten in the bright light.
A new day has begun for the rabbit, the robins,
the old dog, and the boy and the girl.

But not for the owl. He nestles his head on his chest.
He closes one big round eye and then the other.

Sleep tight, Owl.